WHALE SONG

by TONY JOHNSTON

illustrated by ED YOUNG

G.P. Putnam's Sons
New York

For MARGARET and DAVID,
who can count endlessly.
T.J.

To YANG WEI CHENG,
who bent my wayward ear to
the magical world of numbers.
E.Y.

Text copyright © 1987 by Tony Johnston
Illustrations copyright © 1987 by Ed Young
All rights reserved. Published simultaneously in
Canada by General Publishing Co. Limited, Toronto.
Printed in Hong Kong by South China Printing Co.

Book design by Nanette Stevenson
Calligraphy by Jeanyee Wong

Library of Congress Cataloging-in-Publication Data
Johnston, Tony.   Whale song.
Summary: Counting as they sing, whales
use their mighty voices to pass on to one another
the numbers from one to ten.
[1. Whales—Fiction.   2. Counting]
I. Young, Ed, ill.   II. Title.
PZ7.J6478Wh   1987   [E]   86-18653
ISBN 0-399-21402-X

First printing

Some say the whales
sing songs to each other,
across wide oceans, around the world.

I say they are counting.

Far
out in
the middle
of an ocean
a colossal
whale sings,

ONE!

ONE!
ONE!
ONE!

echoes through blue waters
   and bumps into a whale
      swimming in a place
         where mountains are of ice.

TWO!

sings this whale in a great, big, frosty voice.

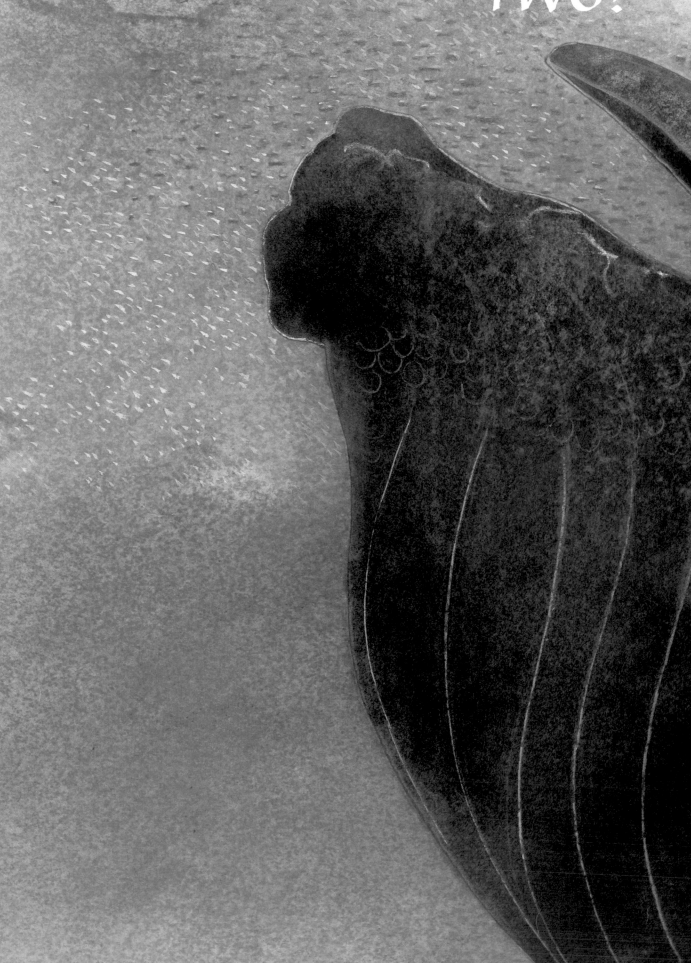

glides along until
    it finds a whale
        big as an island,
            eating lunch
                at the
                    bottom of the sea.

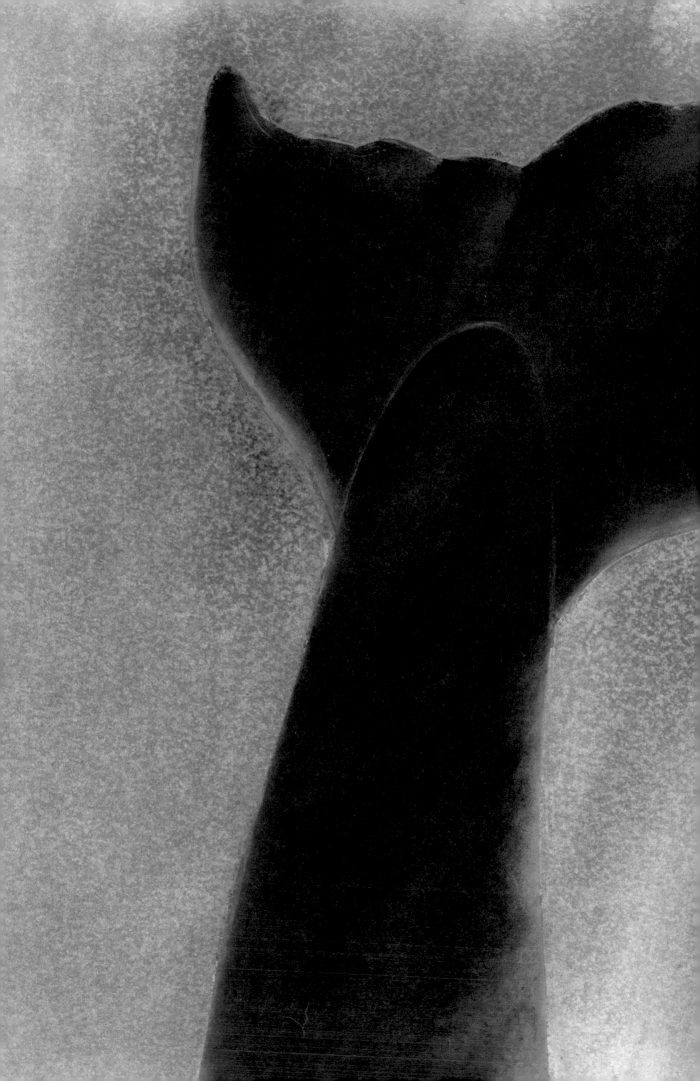

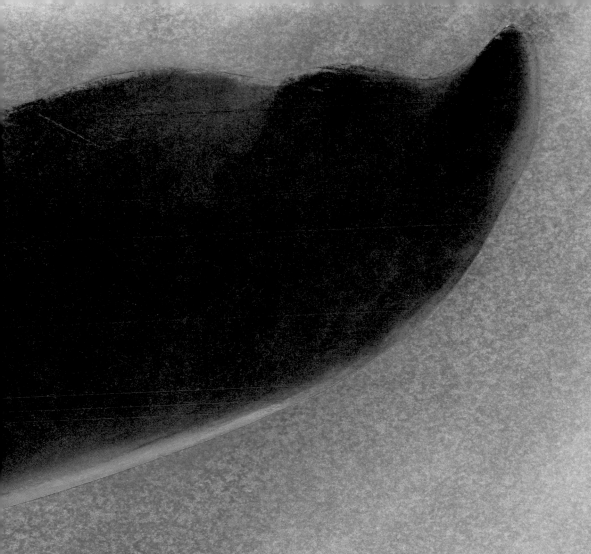

When lunch is done he sings out,

THREE!

meets some
big wet whales
smacking their tails
rolling over and over,
in a rolling, rainy sea.
They keep on rolling
as they sing out.

FOUR!

rolling and singing,
singing and rolling
in the rain.

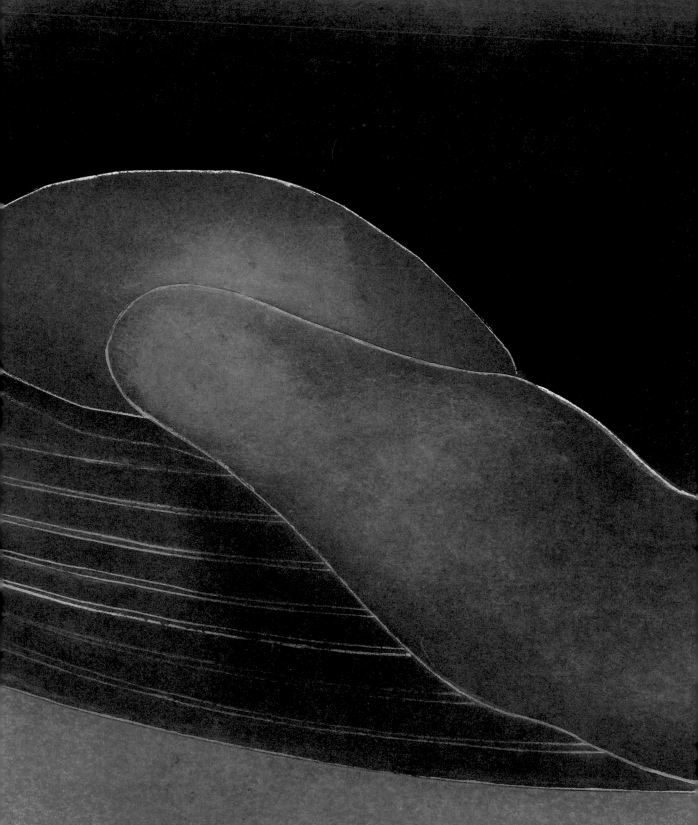

FOUR! ripples through the ocean
like a mighty wave
until it reaches a whale
deep down where seaweed grows
and fishes hide inside.

In a tremendous
voice she sings out, FIVE!

just like an opera singer.

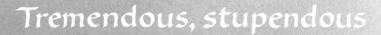

Tremendous, stupendous
FIVE!

rumbles through the water
like a locomotive train
and greets another whale,
a mother whale,
lulling her baby to sleep.

Softly she sings,
SIX, SIX, SIX.
But does her calf sleep?

NO!
He just laughs and sings out,

SEVEN!

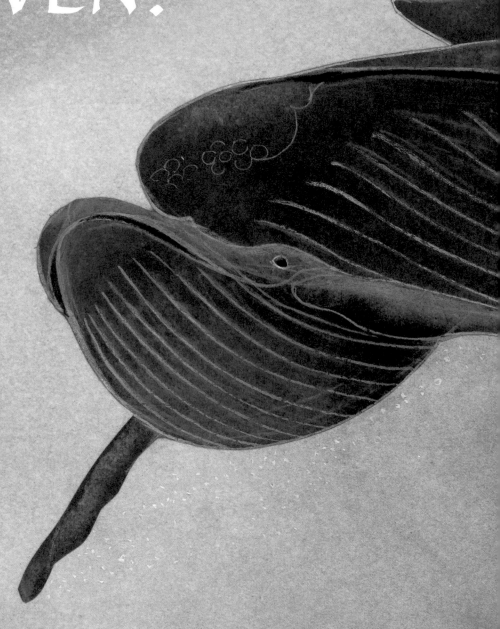

SEVEN!

SEVEN!

SEVEN!

SEVEN! swims through turquoise seas,
and a pod of uncle whales
(just like a pod of peas if you please)
hears it in seas way past the sunset.
The uncles rise up
and sound out,

EIGHT!

Higher and higher,
    an uncle choir.

That EIGHT! goes flying to where
a grandfather whale all crusty with barnacles
is floating along, humming to himself.
He is the oldest of whales
and he loves to count.

He sings out,

NINE!

NINE! NINE! NINE!

Again and again.

There is a silence then.

And all the whales wonder, what comes next?

So, in a voice like thunder,

I shout out,

TEN!